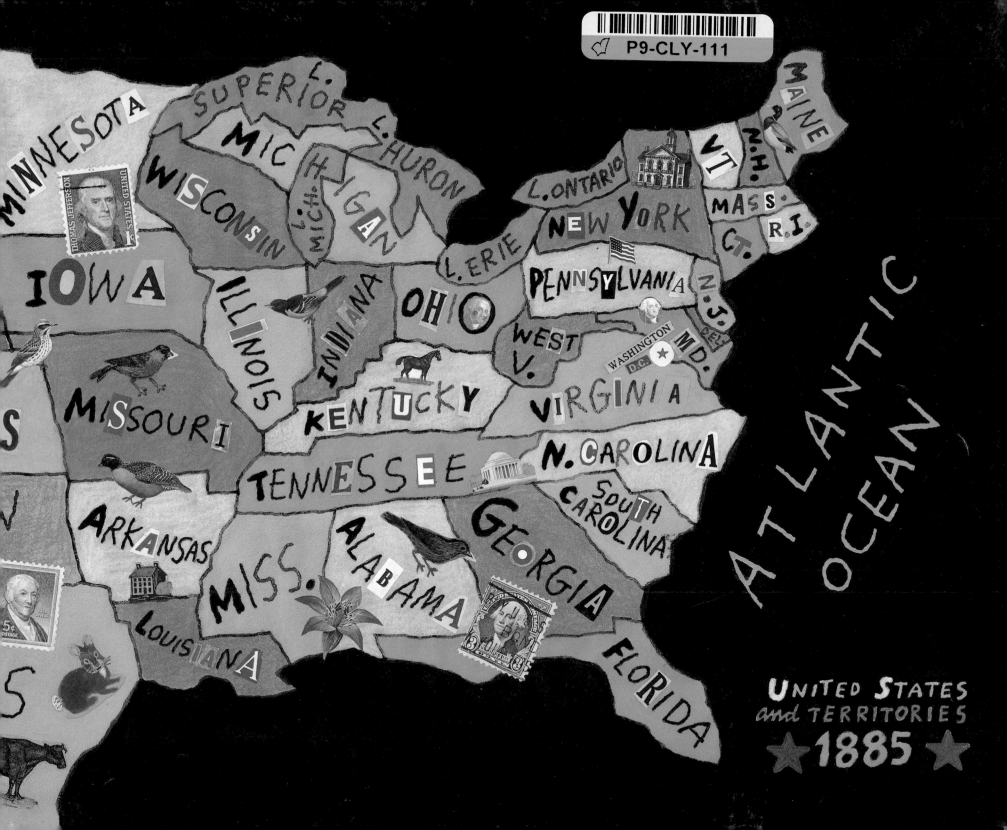

In memory of my grandparents,

who came here from Russia—HMZ

For Leon—ST

"When I First Came to This Land" was brought to Pennsylvania over a century ago by a German immigrant.
It appears in AND THE GREEN GRASS GREW ALL AROUND: FOLK POETRY FROM EVERYONE
by Alvin Schwartz (HarperCollins Publishers, 1992).

Published simultaneously in Canada. Printed in Hong Kong by South China Printing Co. (1988) Ltd.
Text set in Cheltenham Bold
Library of Congress Cataloging-in-Publication Data
Ziefert, Harriet. When I first came to this land / retold by Harriet Ziefert; pictures by Simms Taback. p. cm.
Summary: Illustrations and words to a traditional song describe the adventures of a pioneer who buys
a farm and builds life for himself and his family. 1. Folk songs, English—United States—Texts.
[1. Folk songs—United States.] I. Taback, Simms, ill. II. Title. PZ8.3.Z49Wf 1998
782.42162'13'00833—DC21 97-9612 CIP AC
ISBN 0-399-23044-0
1 3 5 7 9 10 8 6 4 2
First Impression

WHEN I FIRST CAME TO THIS LAND

RETOLD BY HARRIET ZIEFERT
PICTURES BY SIMMS TABACK

G. P. Putnam's Sons   New York

When I first came to this land,
I was not a wealthy man.

But the land was sweet and good,
And I did what I could.

I bought a farm.

And I called my farm
Muscle-in-my-arm!

I borrowed a plow.

I called my plow
Don't-know-how!
And I called my farm
Muscle-in-my-arm!

I bought a horse.

I called my horse
I'm-the-boss!
I called my plow
Don't-know-how!
And I called my farm
Muscle-in-my-arm!

I built a shack.

I called my shack
Break-my-back!
I called my horse
I'm-the-boss!
I called my plow
Don't-know-how!
And I called my farm
Muscle-in-my-arm!

I bought a cow.

I called my cow
No-milk-now!
I called my shack
Break-my-back!
I called my horse
I'm-the-boss!
I called my plow
Don't-know-how!
And I called my farm
Muscle-in-my-arm!

I bought a pig.

I called my pig
Too-darn-big!
I called my cow
No-milk-now!
I called my shack
Break-my-back!
I called my horse
I'm-the-boss!
I called my plow
Don't-know-how!
And I called my farm
Muscle-in-my-arm!

I found a wife.

I called my wife
Spice-of-my-life!
I called my pig
Too-darn-big!
I called my cow
No-milk-now!
I called my shack
Break-my-back!
I called my horse
I'm-the-boss!
I called my plow
Don't-know-how!
And I called my farm
Muscle-in-my-arm!

WANTED—A WIFE,

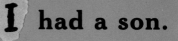 had a son.

I called my son
So-much-fun!
I called my wife
Spice-of-my-life!
I called my pig
Too-darn-big!
I called my cow
No-milk-now!
I called my shack
Break-my-back!
I called my horse
I'm-the-boss!
I called my plow
Don't-know-how!
And I called my farm
Muscle-in-my-arm!

My son found a duck.

And he called his duck
Duck-Duck-Duck!
And he called his pa
Da-Da-Da!
And he called his ma
Ma-Ma-Ma!

When I first came to this land,
I was not a wealthy man.

But the land was sweet and good,
And I did what I could!